The Biggest Pumpkin

The Biggest Pumpkin

By
Sandra Horning

Illustrated by
Holly Stone-Barker

PELICAN PUBLISHING COMPANY
GRETNA 2014

In loving memory of Annie Gladden

Library of Congress Cataloging-in-Publication Data

Horning, Sandra, 1970-
  The biggest pumpkin / by Sandra Horning ; illustrated by Holly Stone-Barker.
    pages cm
  Summary: "Gavin wants to cultivate the biggest pumpkin for the town fair. With the help of friends, neighbors, and family, he achieves his goal, but how will he get it to the fair?"--Provided by publisher.
  ISBN 978-1-4556-1925-2 (hardcover : alk. paper) -- ISBN 978-1-4556-1926-9 (e-book) [1. Pumpkin--Fiction. 2. Growth--Fiction.] I. Stone-Barker, Holly, illustrator. II. Title.
  PZ7.H7867Bi 2014
  [E]--dc23

                    2014000018

Printed in Malaysia
Published by Pelican Publishing Company, Inc.
1000 Burmaster Street, Gretna, Louisiana 70053

The Biggest Pumpkin

"What do you want to enter in the town fair?" Gavin's mom asked.

"A **big pumpkin.**" Gavin reached to the sky to show how big the pumpkin would be.

"You could plant it there." His mom pointed to a small patch of dirt.

"No, I'll need more space," Gavin said. "I'm growing the **biggest** pumpkin. I want to win a prize."

Gavin grabbed his wagon and they walked to McShay's Hardware and Garden Shop.

"I want to grow the **biggest pumpkin** for the fair." Gavin reached to the sky to show how big the pumpkin would be.

"I know just the seed." Mr. McShay picked out a packet. "This grows a mighty **big pumpkin.**"

Gavin plopped down the coins from his piggy bank. "I'm paying for it *myself.*"

"Growing a **big pumpkin** takes lots of work," Mr. McShay said. "I'd plant this right away—early May is the best time to plant this seed."

Gavin nodded. "I'll start today."

At home Gavin planted his pumpkin **seed** in the middle of the yard. Then he watered it.

Every day he watered it. By the end of the first week in May, a tiny green **stem** pushed through the soil.

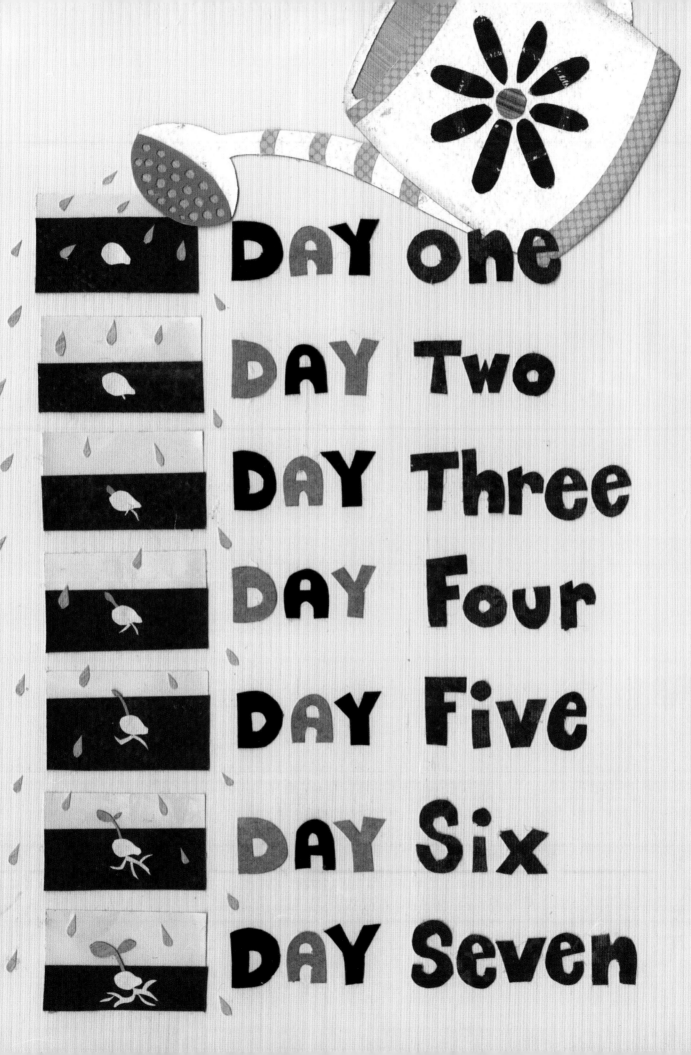

DAY one

DAY Two

DAY Three

DAY Four

DAY Five

DAY Six

DAY Seven

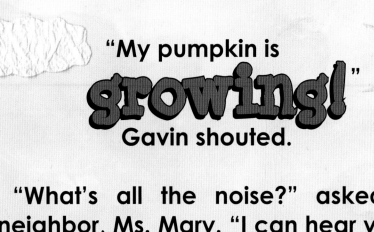

"My pumpkin is **growing!**" Gavin shouted.

"What's all the noise?" asked his neighbor, Ms. Mary. "I can hear you in my kitchen."

"I'm growing the **biggest pumpkin.**" Gavin reached to the sky to show how big the pumpkin would be.

"I was a champion gardener in my day." Ms. Mary's eyes gleamed. "I have a **secret.** Put a little greenhouse over it."

Ms. Mary hurried away and soon returned with supplies. "This will protect it from the **wind** and the **cold** nights we're still having." She and Gavin worked together to build a mini-greenhouse over the plant.

NAILS

Each day Gavin and Ms. Mary checked on the plant. The first week of June, Ms. Mary removed the mini-greenhouse. A few weeks later, the first flowers appeared on the plant.

"Flowers!"

Gavin hollered.

Ms. Mary, Gavin, and Gavin's mom huddled to look closer.

"What's going on?" the mailman asked.

"I'm growing the **biggest** pumpkin." Gavin reached to the sky to show how big the pumpkin would be.

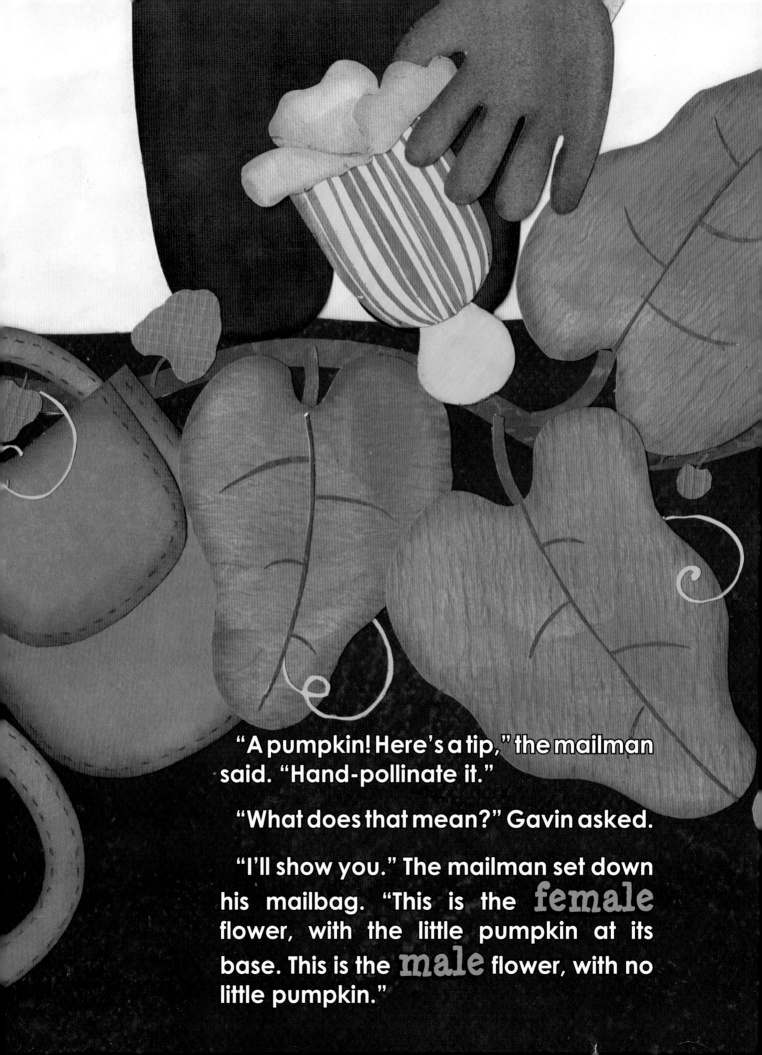

"A pumpkin! Here's a tip," the mailman said. "Hand-pollinate it."

"What does that mean?" Gavin asked.

"I'll show you." The mailman set down his mailbag. "This is the **female** flower, with the little pumpkin at its base. This is the **male** flower, with no little pumpkin."

The mailman picked the male flower.

"Take off the flower petals. See the pollen?" He rubbed the pollen onto the center of the female flower. "Bees do this, but if we do it now, your pumpkin will start growing even sooner."

"This will be the best pumpkin!" Gavin cheered.

Now Gavin, Ms. Mary, and the mailman checked on the plant every day. In early July, several pumpkins were growing on the vines.

"Three pumpkins!"

Gavin yelled.

"Oh, dear," Ms. Mary said. "We want all the plant's energy to go to one pumpkin."

Colby pedaled by on his bike. "Hi, Gavin. What are you doing?"

"Growing the **biggest** pumpkin." Gavin reached to the sky to show how big the pumpkin would be. "We're choosing the best one."

"I want to help!" Colby parked his bike. "My keychain has a tape measure."

They measured the pumpkins and picked all but the 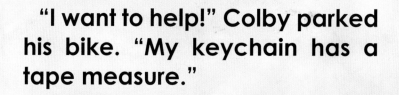biggest one off the vines.

Now Gavin, Ms. Mary, the mailman, and Colby checked on the pumpkin every day.

"I heard you're growing a pumpkin," Aunt Daisy said during a visit in July.

"Not a pumpkin, the **biggest** pumpkin." Gavin reached to the sky to show how big the pumpkin would be.

"Do I have the perfect plant food for you! I blend it with my special **compost** mix," Aunt Daisy said. "I brought some."

  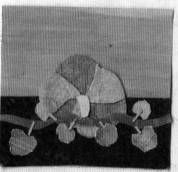 

Aunt Daisy spread her **fertilizer** around the plant's base. "Add some of this each week and your pumpkin will grow even bigger."

Each day the pumpkin grew

bigger and bigger.

In August, it reached the top of Gavin's head. Finally, at the end of September, the day of the fair arrived.

Gavin measured the pumpkin one last time.

"It's **taller** than **me!**"

Gavin and Colby **pushed** and **pushed,** but the pumpkin didn't budge. Gavin's mom, Ms. Mary, and the mailman tried to push with them. They shook their heads.

"That pumpkin won't move," said Ms. Mary.

"And it won't fit in a car either," added the mailman.

Gavin cried, "But the judging is today!"
"I'm sorry, but I don't know how to move it," Gavin's mom said.

Gavin suddenly jumped up. "I know— **Uncle Peter!**"

Soon Uncle Peter arrived with his truck and forklift. He whistled as he loaded the pumpkin into the truck. "Isn't she a **beauty!**"

Slowly, they drove into the town fairgrounds.

"Drive faster, Uncle Peter!" Gavin pleaded.

"You're just in time. This is the last pumpkin to be weighed." The mayor grinned. They lifted it onto the scale. It weighed 501 pounds!

"This is the biggest pumpkin our town has ever seen," the mayor said. "First prize!"

"Hooray! We did it!" Gavin clapped.

"Now let's make the **biggest** jack-o'-lantern. Pumpkin pie for everyone!"

As Gavin and his friends cleaned out the pumpkin, Gavin asked, "Mr. McShay, do you sell giant **watermelon seeds?**"

GLOSSARY

bees. Insects that feed on pollen and nectar. As they do this, they move pollen to other flowers and help them bear fruit.

compost. Leaves, grass, and other organic matter that are left to decay and then used as fertilizer.

fertilizer. A substance added to soil to help plants grow.

flower. The part of the plant where the seed or fruit develops.

pollen. A fine, dustlike material made by a plant, so that it may make seeds.

pollinate. To move pollen from one flower to another.

seed. A small object made by a plant from which a new plant can grow.

stem. The main stalk of a plant.

AUTHOR'S NOTE

In August through October, many towns have harvest fairs. Besides games and rides, these fairs have contests for the biggest and best vegetables grown in the area. Since my house is surrounded by trees, I don't have enough sunlight to grow my own giant pumpkins. Instead, my family and I enjoy visiting the fairs to see them.

The Biggest Pumpkin is fiction, but it really is possible to grow a pumpkin that weighs over 500 pounds. In fact, the heaviest pumpkin in Connecticut, where I live, weighed in at 1,766.5 pounds at the Durham Fair in September of 2013. According to *Guinness World Records*, the heaviest pumpkin in the world was 2,032 pounds! That pumpkin was grown in California in 2013. Maybe someday you can break that record!